ALSO AVAILABLE:

IVY + BEAN BOOK ❶

"The deliciousness is in the details here, with both girls drawn distinctly and with flair." —★*Booklist*, starred review

". . . illustrations deftly capture the girls' personalities and the tale's humor. . . . Barrows's narrative brims with sprightly dialogue."
—★*Publishers Weekly*, starred review

"Readers are bound to embrace this spunky twosome and eagerly anticipate their continuing tales of mischief." —*Kirkus Reviews*

IVY + BEAN AND THE GHOST THAT HAD TO GO BOOK ❷

"This strong follow-up . . . is sure to please." —*Kirkus Reviews*

". . . the series' strong suits are humor and the spot-on take on relationships." —*Booklist*

"This story defies expectations of what an early chapter book can be." —*School Library Journal*

IVY + BEAN BREAK THE FOSSIL RECORD BOOK ❸

"This is a great chapter book for students who have recently crossed the independent reader bridge." —*School Library Journal*

"Just right." —*Kirkus Reviews*

BOOK ❺ COMING SOON!

iVy + BEAN

TAKE CARE OF THE BABYSITTER

BOOK 4

written by annie barrows + illustrated by sophie blackall

chronicle books·san francisco

For Liz and Morgan, babysitter and babysat —A. B.

For Callum and Harrison —S. B.

Band-Aid is a registered trademark of Johnson & Johnson.

Book design by Sara Gillingham.
Typeset in Blockhead and Candida.
The illustrations in this book were rendered in Chinese ink.
Manufactured by Leo Paper Products, Heshan, China, in December 2010.

Library of Congress Cataloging-in-Publication Data
Barrows, Annie.
Ivy and Bean take care of the babysitter / by Annie Barrows ; illustrated by Sophie Blackall.
p. cm.
"Book 4."
Summary: When Bean's parents leave her in the care of her older sister Nancy for the afternoon,
she enlists her neighbor and best friend Ivy to come over and teach Nancy how to be a really good
babysitter.
ISBN 978-0-8118-5685-0
[1. Sisters—Fiction. 2. Babysitters—Fiction. 3. Behavior—Fiction.] I. Blackall, Sophie, ill. II. Title.
PZ7.B27576It 2008
[Fic]—dc22
2007028224

10 9 8 7 6 5 4

This product conforms to CPSIA 2008.

Chronicle Books LLC
680 Second Street, San Francisco, California 94107

www.chroniclekids.com

CONTENTS

TOO GOOD TO BE TRUE

Thwack!

Bean was grinding corn. She put a few pieces of Indian corn on the sidewalk and then smacked a rock down on top of them. *Thwack!* It hardly dented them, but that was okay. That was part of the fun. You had to pound for a long time.

Thwack!

"What are you *doing*?" It was her sister, Nancy, standing on the porch.

"Grinding corn." *Thwack!* Bean looked at her corn. It was dented now. "You can do some, too, if you want. I've got lots of corn."

Nancy watched her pound. "What's it for?"

"Food," said Bean. "I'm making cornbread."

Thwack! "Hey, look! Corn dust!"

Nancy almost came to look. She even took a step down the stairs. But then she got a prissy look on her face and said, "Like Mom's going to let you eat stuff that's been on the sidewalk. Dream on."

Bean could have thrown the rock at her, but she knew better than that. Bean was seven. Nancy was eleven. Bean knew how to drive Nancy nutso without getting into trouble herself. She began to moan loudly, "Grind or starve! Winter's coming! If we don't grind corn, we'll have to eat rocks!"

"Cut it out, Bean!" hissed Nancy. "Everyone will see you!"

Nancy was always worried that everyone would see her. Bean wanted everyone to see her. She lay down on the side-walk and rolled from side to side, moaning, "Just a little corn dust, that's all I ask!"

The front door slammed. Nancy had gone inside. That was easy.

Bean lay on the sidewalk, resting. The sun was warm. She loved Saturdays.

"We've got dirt at my house," said a voice above her.

It was Sophie W. from down the street.

"What kind of dirt?" asked Bean.

Sophie smiled. Both her front teeth were out, and she had filled the hole with gum. "A lot of dirt."

That sounded interesting. Bean jumped up and grabbed her bag of corn. Together, she and Sophie hurried around Pancake Court.

Usually Sophie W.'s house looked a lot like all the other houses on Pancake Court, but today it looked different. Today, there was an enormous mound of dirt in the front yard. A *monster* mound. It was as high as the front porch. Maybe even higher. It spread across most of the lawn, all the way to the path. The dirt was dark brown, the kind of dirt that smells good and is already halfway to mud.

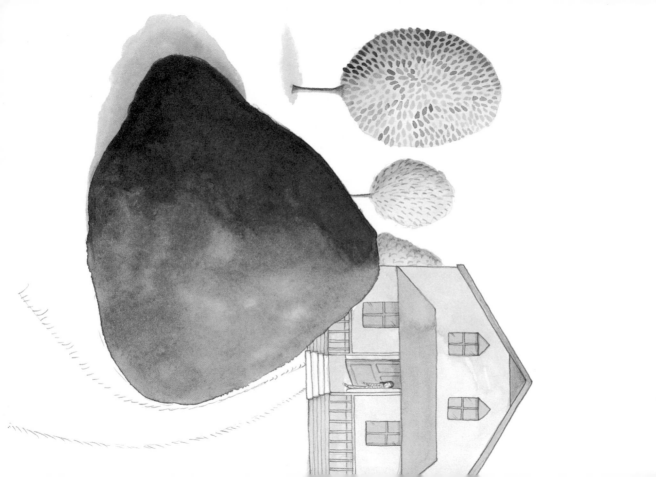

"Wow. Your parents actually gave you dirt?" asked Bean.

"Sort of," Sophie said. "They're going to use it in the backyard, but not until next week."

"We can play on it?" asked Bean. It was too good to be true. "It's okay with your mom?"

Sophie W. looked at her front door and giggled. "My mom's not home! There's a babysitter in there!"

Bean stared at the mound. They wouldn't put it out in the front yard if they didn't want people to use it, she thought. "Shouldn't we ask the babysitter?" she said.

Just at that moment, a teenage girl stuck her head out the front door. She was the babysitter. "Oh," she said to Sophie. "There you are."

"Is it okay if we play with this dirt?" asked Bean politely.

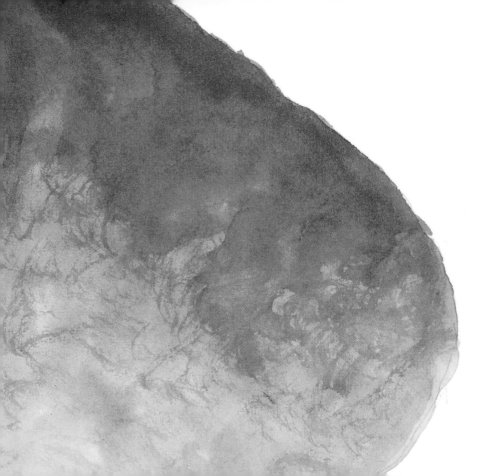

The teenager looked at the mound like she had never seen it before. "I guess. Um. Don't track it into the house."

"No problem," said Bean. "We don't even want to go in the house."

The babysitter nodded and turned to Sophie. "I guess I'll be watching TV, okay?"

"Sure," said Sophie. She and Bean waited until the teenager was inside. Then Sophie turned to Bean. "What should we play?"

"Play?" said Bean. "We haven't got time to play! This volcano's about to blow!"

DISASTER TWINS

Ivy wouldn't want to miss out on a volcano, that was for sure. Bean zipped up the street to Ivy's house and rang the doorbell. But that was too slow. "Hey!" she yelled through the mail slot. "There's a volcano at Sophie W.'s!"

"A what?" said Ivy, opening the door. Ivy was reading. She was reading a really big book with long words even on the cover, which was something Bean couldn't stand. It was bad enough when there were big words inside the book.

"A volcano!" Bean yelled. "Come on!" Ivy looked at her book.

Bean rolled her eyes. "Ivy! It's a natural disaster! You have to be there!"

"Okay," said Ivy. She put down her book.

"You are so weird sometimes," said Bean. "Come on!"

The two girls ran back to Sophie's house. Leo was there now, and Sophie S. and Prairie and Prairie's little brother, Isaiah.

When she got to the front yard, Bean fell onto the grass. "Earthquake!" she hollered.

Volcanoes made the earth shake, too. Volcanoes and earthquakes were like disaster twins.

Ivy grabbed a bush and shook it back and forth to show that the earth was quaking. Sophie W. and Prairie pretended they were being crushed by falling buildings. Leo pretended his car blew up, which was a little strange, but he said it happened all the time during earthquakes.

"Smoke!" screeched Bean, pretending to be terrified. She pointed to the dirt mountain. "She's going to blow!"

They all stopped what they were doing and looked at the mound of dirt.

"It would be better if we had real smoke," said Sophie S.

"It would be better if we had real lava," said Bean.

Ivy glanced around the yard, looking for lava. There wasn't any, but she did see a hose lying on the lawn. Hmmm. She picked it up.

"That's good," said Bean. "Lava flows, just like water."

"Yup," said Ivy. "But how are we going to get it to come out the top of the dirt?"

They all thought about that for a minute.

"I know," said Prairie, her eyes shining. "Let's stick him inside." She pointed to Isaiah. "We dig a hole at the top, and then we bury him with the hose."

Isaiah looked worried.

"If we bury him," said Bean, "he won't be able to breathe."

Isaiah nodded.

"We'll just dig a hole," said Leo. "We won't bury him."

"It'll be like a sacrifice to the gods," said Ivy in a dreamy voice.

"I'm going home," said Isaiah. He ran.

Prairie caught him. She promised to give him her stuffed seal plus three glow-in-the-dark stickers. Also a lollipop the next time she got two. That was a lot, just for being the lava. Isaiah said okay.

It took quite a while to build the volcano. At first, they tried climbing to the top of the mound to dig the crater. A lot of dirt slid off the mound, and so did Ivy and Sophie S.

In the end, they decided to smash down the dirt in the back of the mound to make steps and then dig an Isaiah-sized crater near the top. It would only look like a volcano from the front, but who cared?

Finally, everything was perfect. Isaiah climbed the steps slowly, holding the hose and Bean's bag of corn. Bean, Ivy, Leo, Prairie, and Sophie S. gathered around the foot of the volcano. Sophie W. got to turn on the hose, since it was her house.

"You ready?" called Prairie.

"Yes," said Isaiah. They could hardly hear him inside the crater.

"On your mark!" yelled Bean. "Get set! Go!" She threw herself onto the ground.

"Earthquake!" she bellowed.

"Help!" howled Sophie S. "The volcano is spewing!"

Isaiah threw the corn out the top.

"Ask the gods for forgiveness!" yelled Ivy.

"It's too late!" shouted Leo, flapping bushes back and forth.

"Ohhh nooooo! Here it comes!" hollered Prairie.

Sophie W. laughed and turned the hose on full blast.

"AAAHH!" screamed the volcano, and water blew out the top of the crater in a gigantic spray.

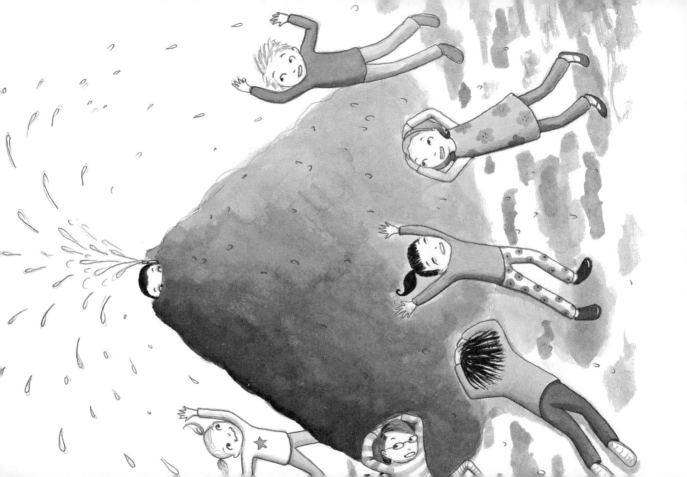

+ + + + + +

Bean was sopping wet. There was corn in her hair. There was mud on her clothes. She was crawling through the burning lava to bring life-giving corn to the hungry townspeople. The hungry townspeople were some rocks over by the edge of the lawn. Ivy and Leo and Prairie and both Sophies were crawling through the burning lava, too. Isaiah refused to come out of the crater.

"BEEE-EEN! TIME TO COME HO-OME!"

It was Bean's mom, calling from her porch.

Weird. Bean had already had lunch. She decided her mother didn't really mean it.

"BEAN! I MEAN NOW!"

Oops. Maybe she did really mean it. Bean stood up. "Five more minutes?" she yelled.

"NOW, BEAN!" Bean's mother sounded cranky.

"I've got to go," Bean said to the other kids.

"Okay," said Ivy. "See you."

"Bye," said Sophie W., pulling a corn kernel out of the mud. "Look! Food!"

Bean looked at them. "You know," she said, "that's my corn. And it was my idea. You guys should stop till I come back."

Leo sat back on his heels. "No way."

"It's my dirt," Sophie W. pointed out.

Bean looked at Ivy. Ivy shrugged. "I want
to keep on playing," she said.

Bean scowled. It wasn't fair. "You wouldn't
even know about it if it wasn't for me." Some
friend *she* was.

"BEEE-EEN!"

Bean stomped home.

THE SPECIAL EXPERIMENT

"What do you want?" Bean said to her mother.

"Excuse me?" said her mother. That meant that Bean had been rude and she'd better shape up quick.

"Sorry. What?"

"Well!" Her mother smiled brightly. "Today we're going to try a special experiment, and I want you to be on your best behavior."

Best behavior? It was Saturday! Bean looked carefully at her mother. She was wearing lipstick. "Where are you going?" Bean asked.

"Daddy and I are going to a play—"

"Can I come?" Bean always asked that, even if she didn't really want to go.

"No. It's for grown-ups," said her mom.

"Is Leona babysitting?" Bean liked Leona. She had long black hair, and she could draw perfect horses.

"No." Bean's mom sighed. "Leona has poison oak. That's the reason for the special experiment."

Bean wasn't liking the sound of this. Grown-ups used the word special when they really meant weird.

"Did you know that I was eleven years old when I started babysitting?" her mom asked.

"No." Uh-oh. Was she about to get a new babysitter?

"Well, I was," her mother went on. "And now that Nancy's eleven, we've decided to let her take care of you for the afternoon."

"What?!" yelped Bean. Nancy was her new babysitter?

"And you'll behave just like you'd behave for any other babysitter," said her father, popping into the room. His hair was wet.

"Which means nicely," said her mother.

"Calmly."

"You're going to let *Nancy* babysit me?" yelled Bean. "She'll kill me!"

"She won't kill you."

"She'll tie me up and stuff me in the attic!" hollered Bean.

"She's not going to tie you up and stuff you in the attic," said her father.

"We don't have an attic," said her mother. "We have a crawl space."

"She won't give me anything to eat! I'll starve!" Bean couldn't stop yelling.

"We're only going to be gone a few hours. We'll

be home for dinner. You won't starve," said her father.

Bean looked from her mom to her dad. They looked back at her. They had already decided, and they weren't going to change their minds. They were really going to leave her with Nancy. Bean had no choice. "Can I go back to Sophie's, at least?" she asked.

"No," said her mom. "That's the other thing, honey. We want you to stay at home this afternoon. Inside the house, where Nancy can keep an eye on you. Just to be on the safe side."

This was getting worse and worse. Bean pressed her hands against her cheeks and rolled her eyes back in her head. She opened her mouth as wide as it would go.

"Bean! Stop that!" said her mother.

Bean stopped it. "Mom," she said, trying to sound calm and nice. "Do you realize that we built a volcano in Sophie W.'s yard? Do you realize that everybody in the whole entire world is down there except me? And it's erupting? And it was my idea?"

"You can call Ivy and ask her to come over if you want," said her mother.

"No, I can't, because she's playing at Sophie's," said Bean grumpily. "Along with everybody else in the whole entire world."

"I'm sorry, honey. It's just for one afternoon." Her mother felt bad; Bean could tell.

Her dad didn't. "You'll live," he said.

Bean collapsed onto the rug. "I'm doomed," she moaned. "I'm double-doomed!"

"Hey, Beanie!" said Nancy, bouncing into the living room. "Did you hear the news? We're going to have a great time! I'll even play crazy eights if you want."

Bean looked up at Nancy with narrow eyes. She was faking. The minute their parents left, Nancy was going to start being the meanest babysitter in the world.

"Okay!" said her dad, slapping his hands together. "Great! Crazy eights! Let's get going, Char! Can't be late!"

Her mom bent down and patted Bean's cheek. "We'll be back in no time, sweetie."

Bean closed her eyes. She hoped she looked like a poor little thing.

"Take good care of your little sister, Nancy," said her mom.

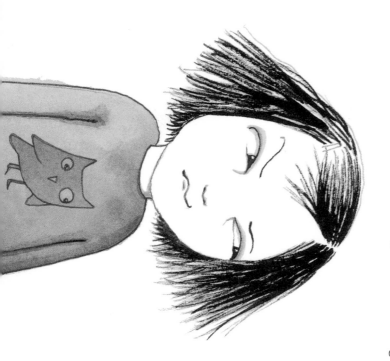

"No worries," Nancy sang. "Have a great time!"

There was the sound of her mother putting on a sweater.

There was the sound of the door closing.

They were gone.

Triple-doomed, thought Bean.

Bean opened her eyes. Nancy was standing

in the doorway. She had her hair up in a bouncy ponytail. She was smiling with lots of teeth, like a camp counselor. "Do you want to play cards?" she said in a peppy voice.

"No," said Bean. "Why are you so happy?"

Nancy's smile got even bigger. "Because I'm getting twenty dollars for this."

WHO'S IN CHARGE?

"I'm the one who should get twenty dollars,"
Bean said. It was about the fifth time she had
said it. "Putting up with you. Teaching you
how to be a babysitter. God!"

"Don't say God," Nancy said. She was
reading a magazine.

"You're not in charge of me!" Bean huffed.

"Actually, I am," Nancy said. But she didn't say it in a mean way. Bean had been trying to make Nancy mad ever since their parents left, but she hadn't been able to. Nancy was being mature. It was driving Bean bonkers.

Bean rolled over and breathed into the rug. She might smother. If she smothered, her parents would feel really bad. Bean picked some rug fuzz out of her mouth. She knew she wasn't going to smother. She also knew that Nancy wasn't going to tie her up and stuff her in the attic. Neither of those things

was the problem. The problem was Nancy being her *babysitter*. That meant that Nancy was the grown-up, the one who got to decide everything. And it meant that Bean was the little, boring, poopy baby who didn't get to decide anything.

Bean couldn't stand it anymore. She got up.

44

"Where are you going?" asked Nancy, looking over her magazine. "You're not supposed to go out."

"What is this—jail?!" huffed Bean. "I'm not a criminal, you know. I can go in the front yard!"

"If you do, I'll tell, and you'll get grounded for a week," said Nancy calmly.

Bean pressed her hands against her cheeks, rolled her eyes back in her head, and opened her mouth as wide as it would go. But Nancy wasn't even looking.

Bean stomped up the stairs as loudly as she could. Nancy didn't say anything. Bean slammed the door to her room. She waited. Nothing. Stupid Nancy.

She flung herself down on her bed. She was a prisoner in her own home. Treated like a criminal by her own flesh and blood. "By my own flesh and blood," muttered Bean. It sounded good.

After a few minutes, she stopped being mad and started being bored. She looked around her room for something to do. She could knit. Except that she liked the idea of knitting more than she liked knitting in real life. Besides, her yarn was in a big knot. She thought about painting, but her watercolors were all the way downstairs. She could make a potholder, but she had already made about thirty of them, and the only colors left were brown and gray. Bean's grandmother loved everything she made, but Bean didn't think even her grandmother would want a brown and gray potholder.

Bean flopped into her basket chair. Ouch. She got up and looked out her window. She had never been so bored in her life. She squeezed all the way to the edge of the window and found out that she could see Sophie W.'s yard.

The mound of dirt was smaller than it had been in the beginning. There was muddy water running down the driveway and into the street. Bean pressed her eyebrow against

the glass. Sophie S. had the hose. She was shooting water straight into the sky. Ivy was off to one side, hunched over a pile of rocks.

Bean frowned. Some friend. She should sense that Bean was in trouble. She should feel it in her bones. Ivy picked up a rock and splatted it down in the mud. Bean squinted and saw that Ivy's lips were moving. She was talking to herself. For some reason, that made Bean feel better. Ivy wasn't really having a great time with the other kids. Ivy was just playing by herself. In fact, Ivy was probably missing her right this minute.

Bean tapped her fingers against the window, thinking. Ivy would come to her rescue if she knew that Bean was imprisoned. Bean was sure of it. Somehow, Bean had to let Ivy know what was going on. Then Ivy could help her escape. Hey! Wait a minute! Bean felt an idea landing in her brain like an airplane. An escape! She was in jail, but maybe she could escape. She had heard of prisoners digging tunnels under their jail cells. Too bad her room was upstairs. If she dug a tunnel, she'd fall right into the kitchen.

Then she looked at the window—that would work! Bean pictured herself climbing out the window on a rope ladder. She pictured Ivy hiding in the bushes below, waiting to help Bean to freedom. A rope ladder. A daring escape. Cool!

51

THE UNDERSHIRT
OF FREEDOM

Bean needed some rope, and she needed something to tie it to. But the first thing she needed was Ivy. Bean looked out the window again. Ivy was dropping another rock into mud. *Splat.* Her lips were still moving. How was Bean going to get her attention? If she screamed out the window, Nancy would hear.

Smoke signals would be perfect, but Bean's mother always said that if Bean used matches, she would live to regret it.

Then Bean remembered a movie she'd seen when she was little. In it, a bunch of raggedy people on an island had waved a flag printed with the letters SOS. Then an airplane had come to rescue them. Bean's mother explained that SOS stood for "Save Our Souls." People write it on flags when they want to be saved—after a shipwreck, for example. Bean didn't see why they didn't write SM, for "Save Me," but she wrote SOS anyway. She wrote it on an old undershirt. Then she taped the undershirt to her flagpole. Okay, it wasn't really a flagpole. It was a long silver pole with a hooked end that opened the window in the bathroom ceiling. It was much taller than Bean, and she wasn't supposed to play with it.

"But this is an emergency," Bean said to herself.

Bean rattled the screen on her window until it fell off. Unfortunately, it fell out the window into the front yard, but there was nothing Bean could do about that. Being extra careful not to smack the pole against the glass, Bean edged her flag over the windowsill. Her SOS undershirt fluttered in the breeze. You'd have to be blind not to notice it.

Hey! There was Ivy, walking along the sidewalk! She was going home! She was about to walk right in front of Bean's house! Bean could have called out, but she had gone to all that trouble, making an SOS flag. She didn't want to waste it. She waved the flag gently back and forth.

Ivy didn't notice.

Bean waved the flag up and down.

Ivy just walked along.

Bean jerked the flag in and out.

Ivy didn't look up.

So Bean threw the pole at her.

It landed with a terrible crash at Ivy's feet.

Ivy squeaked and jumped backward. Then she looked up at the sky. "Wow," she said.

She bent down to touch the pole. "An alien."

"It's not an alien! It's an SOS!" Bean said. Now Ivy saw her. "Oh. Hi. Did you throw that at me? Are you mad at me?"

"No, I'm not mad. Don't you see the flag part? It's an SOS. See the letters?"

Ivy looked at the pole again. "Cool." She came to stand under Bean's window. "How come you need to be saved?"

"Because of Nancy," Bean said. "My mom and dad let her *babysit* me."

Ivy looked shocked. "She's not a babysitter. She's your sister."

"And she's getting *twenty dollars* for it!"

Ivy looked even more shocked. "That's totally not fair."

"That's what I said. But nobody ever listens to me."

Talking to Ivy, Bean began to see just how unfair it really was. Super-duper unfair.

"Did she lock you in your room?" Ivy asked.

"Well, no," admitted Bean. "But she won't let me go outside. I'm a prisoner in my own home."

"Do you want some food?" asked Ivy. "You could pull it up in a basket."

"No. I don't want food. I want freedom," said Bean dramatically. "I'm going to escape down a rope ladder."

"Neat-o," said Ivy. "Can I help?"

"Do you have any rope?" asked Bean.

"For sure! I'll go get some!" Ivy whirled around, ready to run.

"Wait!" Bean said. "Listen. I'm going to have to sneak you in." Of course, her mother had said that Ivy could come over, but it was much more fun to sneak. It seemed more like a real jail that way. "So come around to the back door when you've got the rope."

"Okay! I'll meow like a cat. That's how

you'll know it's me." Ivy gave a little hop.

Bean nodded. "Okay. And then we'll have to find a way to get past Nancy."

Ivy was already running toward her house.

WHERE ARE YOU, MISS PEPPY-PANTS?

Bean was a spy. Pressing her back against the wall, she moved down the hall without making a sound. It was harder to be a spy on the stairs because the handrail poked her in the back. Still, she was pretty quiet.

When she got to the bottom of the stairs, she edged silently toward the living room and peeked around the door. But Nancy wasn't there. Hmm. Maybe the kitchen. She slithered toward the door. Empty.

Where was Nancy?

Bean got a little bit of a funny feeling. What if Nancy was gone?

"Nancy?" she said softly.

There was no answer.

"Nancy?" she said in a regular voice. Nothing. "Nancy?"

"I'm in here." Nancy was in the bathroom.

"Don't come in."

Bean went down the hall and stood outside the bathroom door. "What are you doing?" she asked.

"Nothing. None of your business. Don't come in." Nancy's voice was tight. She didn't sound like a camp counselor anymore.

"Are you going to throw up?" Bean asked sympathetically. She knew what that was like.

"No! Go away!" Nancy clicked the lock on the door.

What happened to Miss Peppy-Pants? wondered Bean. What was Nancy *doing* in there? Quietly Bean pressed her ear to the door. She could hear water running, but she could also hear other sounds. *Click. Click. Rattle.*

"Bean? Is that you?" said Nancy from inside the bathroom.

Bean didn't say anything. She was perfectly quiet.

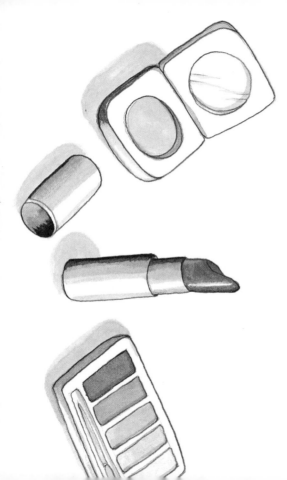

Click. Swish. Spray. The sound of a glass bottle being put down.

All of a sudden, Bean knew. This bathroom was where Bean's mom kept her makeup. Nancy was not supposed to mess around with her mother's makeup. Bean's mother had told Nancy about a thousand times that she was too young to wear makeup. Nancy always said that everyone wore it. Then Bean's mom said that if everyone put their head in the fire, that still wouldn't make it a good idea. Then

Nancy usually cried. They had this conversation a lot.

Now Nancy was in the bathroom putting on makeup.

Some babysitter. She was supposed to be keeping Bean safe and good, and instead she was in the bathroom being bad herself. Bean was just about to point this out when she heard a squeaky meow on the back porch.

Ivy had arrived.

Since Nancy was locked in the bathroom, she probably couldn't hear Ivy come in. But they sneaked anyway. Ivy took off her shoes, and they slid silently across the kitchen and through the hall. Without a word, they tiptoed upstairs and into Bean's room, closing the door behind them.

"Well?" said Bean. "Did you get the rope?"

"Sort of," said Ivy. She looked worried. "It's not exactly rope." She reached into her pocket and pulled out a bundle of string. It was thick string, but it was definitely string.

They both stared at it.

"It was all I could find," Ivy said.

"I guess I could try it," said Bean. But she knew

she wouldn't. It was string. If she made a ladder out of it, it would snap in two, and she would plunge to the ground and break both her legs. Dang. A perfectly good idea down the drain.

"We could throw your mattress out the window and then try to land on it," Ivy suggested.

"We'd miss," said Bean gloomily.

They were quiet for a minute.

"Where is Nancy, anyway?" asked Ivy.

"She's in the bath-room," said Bean.

"She's putting on my mom's makeup." Bean flopped down on her bed and looked at the ceiling. "She told me to go away."

"My babysitters aren't allowed to do that," said Ivy. "They're supposed to play with me, even though I usually don't want them to."

"Oh, she's only doing it because my mom's not here," said Bean. "My mom doesn't let her wear makeup."

"Gee. Nancy's pretty sneaky," said Ivy.

"Yeah. I bet she's been planning it for a million years. The second my mom leaves—boom! She's in the bathroom rubbing eye shadow all over her face."

"That's stupid. Eye shadow's goony," said Ivy.

"Yeah. If I could do anything I wanted, it wouldn't be dumb old eye shadow," said Bean.

"What would you do?" asked Ivy.

"Easy. I'd go in the attic."

"You have an attic?" asked Ivy.

"Yeah, but I've never been in it. My parents won't let me up there," said Bean. "They say it's not really an attic and there's nothing up there and it's too dangerous."

There was a pause.

"Bean?"

"What?"

"Your parents aren't here."

Bean sat up. She pictured the attic, dark, unknown, secret. "If they aren't here, they can't say no!"

"And Nancy did tell you to go away," added Ivy.

"The attic is definitely away." said Bean.

Ivy smiled. "She practically ordered us to go there. Come on!"

THE DOOR IN THE CEILING

There was no reason, Bean told herself, why Nancy should have a good day while she had a bad one. She had been waiting her whole entire life to see the attic. "And besides," she whispered to Ivy as they tiptoed down the hall, "if there's nothing up there, how can it be dangerous?"

"Exactly," whispered Ivy. "Where are the stairs?"

"There aren't any stairs," said Bean. She opened the hall closet. "We go this way." She closed the door behind them and pointed at the ceiling. "See?"

Ivy looked up, up the shelves of sheets and towels to a square wooden door set in the closet ceiling.

"My mom says it's not an attic," Bean said. "She calls it a crawl space."

"Crawl space," said Ivy. "Sounds like something's crawling around up there. Like a monster with slimy arms that drip down to the floor."

Bean didn't like the sound of that. "My mom says there's nothing up there."

"Well of course she'd say that," Ivy said. "Parents never want you to know anything."

"It's my house," Bean said. "I should know what's in it." She looked up to the door in the ceiling. "Maybe there's another kid up there."

"Or some old dolls," said Ivy.

Bean wiggled with excitement. "There could be anything! Let's get going!" She put her foot on the first shelf. It wasn't as sturdy as she expected. It bent in the middle. She gripped the shelf above—the one that held a lot of washcloths—and pulled herself up. It was harder to hang on to a shelf than a tree branch. Shelves were too smooth. She climbed one shelf higher. Hello, wrapping paper. She tried not to step on the fancy white tablecloth, but she did, just a little. Another shelf. Ugly green towels she had never seen before.

Bean looked up. The wooden square was getting closer. She looked down. The floor was far away. Ivy waved. "You're doing great."

"Aren't you coming?" asked Bean.

"Oh. Sure." Ivy stepped onto the bottom shelf. "Gosh. It bends." She took a deep breath, caught hold of the washcloth shelf, and pulled herself up. "You guys have a lot of towels."

"Uh," Bean grunted. She was concentrating. She climbed past a bowl of fake fruit and bonked her head on the ceiling. "Ow." Holding on to the shelf as tight as she could, she looked up. The door to the attic wasn't really a door. It was a square of wood in a frame. It didn't have a handle or hinges or anything.

Bean leaned out, trying not to look down, and pushed against the wood square with her hand. Nothing happened.

"What's going on up there?" said Ivy.

"Can't get it open," Bean puffed.

"Scooch over." Now Ivy was leaning out, too. "We'll push at the same time. One."

"Two," they said together.

"Three!" They bashed the wooden square as hard as they could.

The door leaped upward and thumped down somewhere in the darkness above them. From the open hole, black, lumpy dirt rained down on Bean and Ivy and all the towels and sheets in the closet.

Bean began to cough. "What is this stuff?" Ivy was trying to blink the dirt out of her eyes. "Your parents probably put it there to stop us. Like they use poisonous snakes to guard treasure."

"Dirt won't stop us," Bean said. "We like dirt!"

"Nothing will stop us!" said Ivy.

Bean reached out and grabbed the edge of the opening. A pile of dirt fell on her face. She ignored it. With her feet, she pushed herself up until her top half was inside the attic.

There was a silence.

"Well?" said Ivy.

"I think we're the first people who have ever been in here," said Bean.

"Really? What does it look like?"

Bean's voice echoed from above. "Well, it's empty, and there are lots of boards poking up

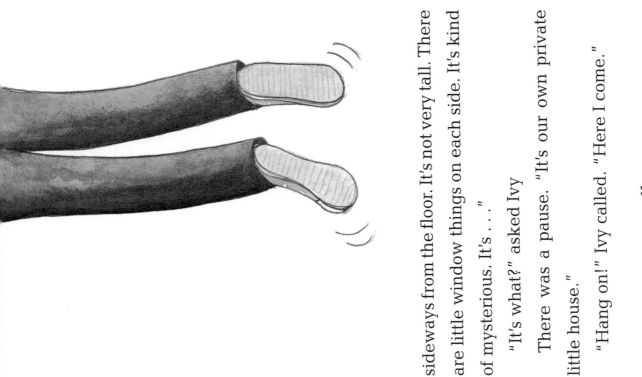

sideways from the floor. It's not very tall. There are little window things on each side. It's kind of mysterious. It's . . ."

"It's what?" asked Ivy

There was a pause. "It's our own private little house."

"Hang on!" Ivy called. "Here I come."

UH-OH

"They'll never figure it out. Not in a million years," Bean was saying. "We'll just disappear and then—ta-da!—we'll come back a few hours later, and they'll have no idea where we've been." She put the door back into its hole and turned to Ivy. "It'll be our secret fort."

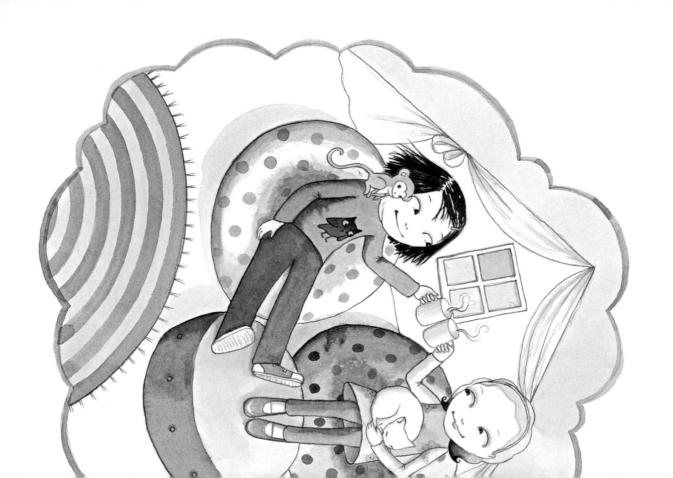

Ivy was moving into the shadows. "We'll fix it up so it's all comfy and cozy. With silk curtains and rugs and poofy pillows."

Bean walked carefully across the boards. "Right over here we could put a little stove, so we could make hot chocolate," Bean said. "We could have a cat, too. And maybe one of those tiny monkeys."

"We could get beds and have secret sleepovers," Ivy went on. Her mother didn't let her have sleepovers yet. "I could sneak out of my house and come over here—"

"And I'll tie a string to my toe and dangle the string out the window. You pull on the string to wake me up, and I'll let you in, and we'll come up here. Oh, I know! Instead of beds, we could put up hammocks, like a ship." Bean hugged herself. It was such a great idea. "And they'll never know. They'll say, 'Where have you been?' and we'll say, 'Us? We were right here.' And it won't be a lie!"

"And when we grow up and they think we're in college, we'll live here," said Ivy. "We'll go out at night to gather food."

"We'll cut a hole in the wall and go out on the roof," said Bean. "After the attic, the thing I want most is to go on the roof."

Ivy got up and knocked on the wall. She could hear outside sounds through the wood. "We could make a balcony," she said. "Our own secret balcony on our own secret house."

"It's going to make Nancy wacko," Bean giggled. "She's going to explode from jealousy when she finds out."

"But you aren't going to tell her, right?"

"Oh. Right. Maybe when we're really old."

Ivy put her hands on her hips. "The first thing we need is silk curtains," she said.

"I don't think we have any silk curtains," Bean said. "But how about some sheets? We've got plenty of extra sheets."

"Sure. For now, we'll use sheets," Ivy agreed.

"Okay. They're in the closet. I'll get them." Bean jumped up and moved away through the shadows.

Ivy thought about rugs and poofy pillows. A lamp would be nice, too.

"Ivy?"

"Yeah?"

"We have a problem."

"What kind of problem?" asked Ivy.

"There's no handle on this door."

"I know," said Ivy. "You just push it."

"Not from this side," said Bean. "Only from the outside."

Uh-oh. Bean had put the door back into the hole. "Can you pull it?" Ivy asked.

"There's nothing to pull."

Ivy stepped carefully across the floorboards and squatted next to Bean. Bean was trying to dig her fingernails around the edge of the door so she could lift it up. But that didn't work because she always chewed her fingernails right down to the skin. Even though Ivy didn't chew her nails, they were still too short to lift the door.

Bean kicked it, but that didn't do anything. Ivy looked for a stick to pry it up with. But there weren't any sticks.

There was no way to open the door.

Bean looked up at the little window things. It was late. Pretty soon, the attic would be completely dark. Nobody knew where they were. They would never figure it out. Not in a million years. She looked around at the empty space with its bare floorboards. It didn't look like a fort anymore. It looked like an attic. Or maybe a jail.

She poked Ivy's arm. "At least you're here, too."

Ivy and Bean sat down side by side and began to wait.

A WORLD OF TROUBLE

"We're going to starve," said Bean.

"I guess we could eat spiders," said Ivy.

"Birds do it."

Bean shivered. She didn't want to eat spiders. All those hairy legs.

They were quiet.

Now that she had started, Bean couldn't stop thinking about spiders. "Ivy?"

"Yeah?"

"Do you ever worry that there's a giant spider who's the grandma of all the spiders you've ever squashed and that she's going to come and get you in the middle of the night?"

"I worry that there's a big potato bug inside my bed," said Ivy. "Not spiders so much."

Bean squinted into the shadows. There were probably spiders crawling all over the attic. Spiders she couldn't see. Something brushed against her leg, and Bean jumped to her feet.

"This is an emergency," said Bean. "This calls for action."

"Okay," agreed Ivy. "What action?"

Bean gulped. "I think we need to scream for help."

"Help from who?" asked Ivy.

"Well," said Bean. "Nancy."

"She *is* the babysitter," said Ivy. "She's supposed to take care of you."

"Right!" said Bean. "She's getting *paid*

to take care of me."

"Okay," said Ivy. "Let's yell for her. One."

"Two," said Bean.

"Three!" they said together. And then they screamed,

ANCYY!

They had to scream for a million years. That's what it felt like anyway. Finally, they heard Nancy. Nancy was yelling, too.

"BEAN? WHERE ARE YOU? WHAT'S HAPPENED? ARE YOU ALL RIGHT?" They could hear doors slamming and Nancy's feet running. "ARE YOU OKAY? ARE YOU IN THE BATHROOM?"

Once Bean knew that she was going to be rescued, she stopped feeling spiders on her legs. After a minute, it was even kind of fun to hear Nancy freaking out. Bean felt cheerful again.

"I've got an idea," she said, "Let's scream, but no words this time, just a scream."

"She's going to have a heart attack," Ivy said.

"AAAAAAHHHHHH," they screeched.

"OH NO!" Nancy shrieked.

Bean took a deep breath and screeched, "WE'RE STUCK IN THE ATTIC! HELP!"

"Bean! Where are you?" Nancy opened the closet door.

"WE'RE UP HERE! HELP!"

"You're up there?" said Nancy in a surprised voice. "How'd you get up there?" Suddenly she didn't sound very worried.

"HELP US! WE'RE STARVING! BUGS ARE EATING US!" hollered Bean.

"Is that Ivy, too?" Nancy asked. "What's she doing here?" Nancy was beginning to sound more grumpy than scared.

Ivy and Bean looked at each other.

"HELLLLLP!" they howled.

"Okay, okay. I'm getting the ladder," grumbled Nancy. "Hang on." She padded away and came back a minute later. "Sheesh. This thing is heavy."

"Quiiiick," moaned Bean. "We're dying." She wanted Nancy to be *leaping* up the ladder.

Something crashed into something else below them. "Ouch!" said Nancy. Then she said a bad word.

Ivy and Bean giggled.

Clump, clump. Nancy climbed up the ladder. *Whack!* The door in front of them popped open—and then Nancy poked her head into the crawl space. "Wow," said Nancy, looking around. "I've never been up here. Is there anything good in here?"

Bean nudged Ivy. "Nothing," she said. "Not a ding-dang thing."

"You wouldn't like it," said Ivy.

Nancy's eyes scanned the darkness and then zipped back to Bean and Ivy. "You're not allowed to go in the crawl space, Bean, and you know it."

Uh-oh, thought Bean. She had hoped Nancy would be so glad to see them that she would forget about that. She tried to look sad. "I was scared," she said in a quavery voice.

"That's your own fault, bozo," said Nancy firmly. "Get down from there."

Nancy climbed down the ladder into the closet. Ivy edged out of the hole and followed her. Bean rolled over onto her stomach, pulled the door toward her, and set it in its frame as she backed down the rungs of the ladder.

Then Nancy noticed the sheets and towels. "What's all this black stuff on the towels? Bean, did all this stuff fall out of the crawl space?"

"I don't see any black stuff," said Bean, stalling.

"Bean, look! It's everywhere," snapped Nancy.

Yikes, thought Bean. There was an awful lot of dirt. More than she

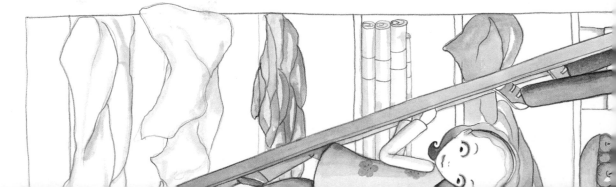

remembered.

"Maybe it was like that before," suggested Ivy.

"It was *not* like this before!" Nancy said. She turned to Ivy. "I don't even know what you're doing here, Ivy!" She whirled around to glare at Bean. "You are going to be in a world of trouble when Mom gets home."

A world of trouble. Bean opened her mouth, but nothing came out.

Then Ivy said in a quiet voice, "My babysitters play with me."

That's it! thought Bean. Maybe she hadn't been exactly good, but that was because Nancy had been a bad babysitter. "Leona always knows where I am," she remarked, "because she's always with me."

Nancy stopped glaring and started looking guilty.

"Leona doesn't sit in the bathroom putting on makeup all afternoon," Bean pointed out. "She earns her money, drawing horses for me."

Nancy made a throat-clearing sound. She brushed some dirt from a towel, and then she gave Bean her big, peppy smile. "You know what?" she said. "I bet I could just vacuum all this

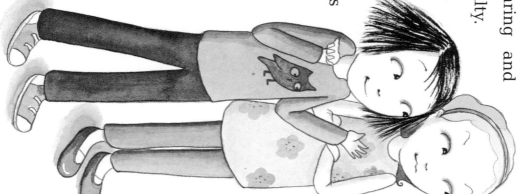

dirt off the sheets and towels. I bet it would come right off."

Bean smiled back at her. "I'll go get the vacuum if you want."

"Okay. You go get the vacuum while I put the ladder away."

ONE IS SILVER AND
THE OTHER'S GOLD

Ivy and Bean were playing in the living room when Nancy finally finished vacuuming. They were playing doll babysitters. Bean's doll was the kid. She had crawled out on the roof and was dancing on the chimney. Ivy's doll was the babysitter. She was having a fit.

"Come down before you fall," wailed Ivy's doll.

"Maybe I will, and maybe I won't," said Bean's doll. Suddenly there was an earthquake. The house was a tall stack of books. Bean's doll fell quite a ways.

"Oh no! My legs are broken!" shouted Bean's doll.

"Luckily, I'm a doctor!" Ivy's doll jumped up. "Let's put Band-Aids on them."

"Too late! The volcano next door is erupting!"

"Here comes the lava! It lifts the house up, and carries it for miles!" Ivy picked up the attic book and threw it across the room. "The babysitter is buried in rubble!"

Nancy walked into the living room looking crabby. "What a mess! You two can just pick up all those books yourselves. I'm tired of cleaning up after you!"

"But we're playing!" said Bean.

"Well, stop playing and pick up those books," snapped Nancy. "I want this place looking perfect when Mom and Dad come home." She glanced at the clock. "Which is going to be soon."

"That's not fair!" Bean started yelling. "We're having fun—" Suddenly she stopped. Nancy looked weird. Her eyelids were silver, and her eyelashes were blue. She had forgotten to wash the makeup off.

"Have you looked in the mirror lately?" asked Bean.

"You're colorful," said Ivy.

Nancy ran down the hall to the bathroom. She banged the door shut. Bean heard the water running.

"I guess we don't have to pick up now," said Ivy.

"She'll still make us do it in a few minutes," sighed Bean.

"My babysitters clean up for me," said Ivy.

"So does Leona, but Nancy's not a real babysitter," said Bean. She tossed her doll onto the floor. Playing was no fun once you knew you had to clean it up. She missed Leona. What if Nancy was going to be her babysitter forever? Her parents would like it, and Nancy would like it, too, because of the money. Ugh. Bean couldn't let that happen.

"I have an idea," said Bean. "Come on." She got up and walked down the hall, and Ivy followed. Bean leaned close to the bathroom door and said loudly, "If it weren't for me, you'd be in big trouble."

Nancy opened the door. Her face was wet and blotchy. "What?"

"It's pretty lucky for you that Mom didn't come in and see that silver stuff," Bean said.

Nancy stared at her for a moment. "Okay. Thanks," she said.

Bean leaned against the doorway. "It's almost like I'm the babysitter," she said.

"You are not!" said Nancy. "I'm the baby-sitter!"

"But I'm keeping you out of trouble like a babysitter," explained Bean.

Nancy opened her mouth, but she didn't say anything.

"That's pretty nice of me, I think. And when we were in the attic, you didn't even know it because you were down here," said Bean.

"Anything could have happened to us." Ivy nodded.

"But you're fine," argued Nancy.

"But I had to take care of myself," Bean said.

"What do you want, Bean?" asked Nancy with narrow eyes.

"Money," said Bean. "Since I was a baby-sitter, I should get some of your money."

"What?!" yelled Nancy. "Why should I give you money? I had to do all that vacuuming!"

"But if you had been paying attention, we wouldn't have been in the attic and you wouldn't have had to vacuum," Bean said. "I think you should give me five dollars."

"No way!"

Bean shook her head. "Mom's going to be mad about the makeup."

Nancy looked like she wanted to slam the door, but she didn't. "I'll give you a dollar," she said finally.

"Five," said Bean.

"Two," said Nancy.

"Four," said Bean.

"Deal," said Nancy. "You promise not to tell? And you, too, Ivy?"

"We promise," said Bean. "Right, Ivy?"

"Right," agreed Ivy.

Nancy looked at the two girls for a moment. "From now on, I'm only babysitting kids who can't talk," she said and slammed the bathroom door shut.

Ivy and Bean walked back down the hall.

"That's two dollars for each of us," said Bean.

"I think I'll buy a doll baby."

"Me, too," said Ivy. "We can have twins."

JUST DESSERTS

A tornado had just hit doll land when Bean's mom opened the front door.

"Hi, sweetie!" said her mother. "How did it go? Where's Nancy? Hi, Ivy."

"Hi," said Bean. "It was fine. I don't know where Nancy is."

"Hi," said Ivy. She made a sound like a siren. "Here come the firefighters!"

"There you are!" said Bean's mom as Nancy came into the living room. "How was it, honey?"

Nancy took a deep breath.

Bean looked up at her.

"I think I'm too young to babysit, Mom," Nancy said.

Bean's mom looked worried. "Why, sweetie?" She turned to Bean. "Bean? Did you misbehave?"

"Me?" Bean said with wide eyes. "I was perfect!"

"Why don't you want to babysit again, honey?" said Bean's mom. She turned to Nancy and brushed her hair out of her face.

"I just don't like it," Nancy said. "I was nervous the whole time."

"Nervous? What were you nervous about?" asked Bean's mom.

Bean wrapped her fingers around her own neck and dangled her tongue out of her mouth.

Nancy saw her. "I was just nervous. I think I'll wait until I'm older before I babysit again."

"Too bad," said Ivy. "I thought you were a great babysitter. I was hoping you could babysit for me one day."

"NO!" said Nancy.

"Nancy!" said Bean's mom. "I think Ivy's being very nice. You don't have to babysit if you don't want to, but you may not be rude."

Nancy clenched her fists into balls and looked at the ceiling. "I am being driven out of my mind!"

"Maybe you need to take some time in your room then," said Bean's mom sternly.

"Fine!" Nancy stomped off down the hall.

Bean's mom looked after her for a moment and then turned to Ivy and Bean. "Did something happen while we were gone?"

"Happen?" saidBean. "Nothing happened."

"Not a thing," said Ivy.

+ + + +
+ +
+

The two girls finished playing. They lay on the floor, relaxing among the books and dolls.

"You know," said Ivy, "I wish Nancy *would babysit me.*"

"Yuck," said Bean. "Why?"

"I could use two more dollars," said Ivy. "I want to buy some dirt so I can make my own volcano, like Sophie W.'s."

"Oooh, that's better than a doll baby!" said Bean. "Let's use our money for dirt!"

"We should be able to buy a lot of dirt for four dollars," said Ivy. "I want it to go all the way up to my porch so I can jump into the crater."

"Cool!" said Bean. "Tomorrow's Sunday. We have a whole day to make a volcano!"

Ivy looked at the ceiling. "I wish we could make a tornado, too."

"Yeah, that would be fun." Bean thought for a moment. "You know," she said, "my dad has a leaf blower."

"Oh boy," Ivy wiggled happily. "We can blow your playhouse over."

Bean's mom came into the living room. "I just called your mom, Ivy. She says you can stay for dinner if you want."

"Yes!" yelled Ivy and Bean at the same time. Bean's mom smiled. "Smart move. We're having cream puffs for dessert."

122

"We are?" asked Bean. She loved how the cream came shooting out onto both sides of her face when she took a bite. "How come?"

"Oh, to celebrate Nancy's first time as a babysitter," said her mother.

"And to celebrate how good Ivy and I were," added Bean. "Right?"

"Right. That too," said Bean's mom. She left the room.

Bean leaned close to Ivy and whispered, "Can you believe how great this day turned out?"

"And there are still lots of hours left," said Ivy.

THE END

SNEAK PREVIEW OF THE NEXT
IVY & BEAN ADVENTURE

Check. Bean's mom was reading the paper.

Check. Bean's dad was reading the paper.

Check. Nancy was reading the funnies.

Bean picked up her plate and licked the streaks of leftover syrup.

"Bean's licking her plate," said Nancy.

"Stop it, Bean," said Bean's mom without even looking up from the paper.

Bean sat on her hands and stared at her plate with her lips shut tight. Then, suddenly, her tongue shot out of her mouth and her head zoomed down to her plate. "I can't help it," she said, licking. "There's a magnetic force pulling my tongue out of my mouth."

All three of them were looking at her like she was a bug. An ugly bug.

"That's disgusting," said Nancy.

"Bean, please . . ." said her mother.

"Cut it out," said her father.

"The force is too strong!" slurped Bean. Her father took her plate away. Bean slumped against the back of her chair. "Thanks dude. I owe you one."

"Don't call me dude," said her dad. "You're doing the dishes."

"What?! It's Nancy's turn!" yelped Bean.

"It was Nancy's turn until you licked your plate. Now it's your turn," said her dad.

"That's totally unfair!" huffed Bean. "I couldn't help it! Haven't you ever heard of forces beyond your control?"

"Yes," said her dad. "That's exactly what's going to make you do the dishes. Get moving."

Bean clumped into the kitchen.

"Bean, you didn't see my pink yarn, did you?"

Oops. Bean tried to roll behind the couch, but Nancy saw her.

"Bean! Do you have my pink yarn?"

"No," said Bean. That was true. She didn't have it. She would never have it again.

Nancy looked at her, slitty-eyed. "Do you know where it is?"

"No." Who knew where it was, by now?

Nancy's eyes got even slittier. "Have you seen it recently?"

"Recently?"

"Mom! Bean took my yarn!"

And before she knew it, Bean was having to look around her room for her money (she changed hiding places so often that it was hard to remember where she kept it, exactly). She had to give Nancy seven dollars to buy new yarn. Seven dollars! Now she only had two dollars and some coins left.

And the yarn hadn't even worked. Bean had fallen out of the tree anyway.